tiffly on the edge of a straight chair, nor sprawl at length in an easy one. ❧ "Keep your hands to

lk at the top of your head, nor at the top of your lungs. ❧ The proper handshake is made briefly;

same time look into the countenan   ne takes. ❧ A handshake often

l extended as though it were a spray of sea-wee   oiled pudding? ❧ Best Society

t might better be described as an unlimited brotherhood which spreads over the entire surface of the

ly perfect manners but a perfect manner. ❧ Elbows are never put on the table while one is eating.

st never be held flat on the palm of the hand and buttered in the air. ❧ All rules of table manners

noise is to suggest an animal; to make a mess is disgusting. ❧ People who have beautiful table

rrible mess. ❧ Birds are not eaten with the fingers in company! You cut off as much of the meat

to your next door neighbor at a dinner table. You must, that is all there is about it! ❧ A small

ome in. If it is her birthday and other children bring her gifts, she must say "Thank you" politely.

st learn at an early age that as hostess she must think of her guests rather than herself, and not

ntest. ❧ The letter you write, whether you realize it or not, is always a mirror which reflects your

he loser, or exulting when the winner, has no right to take part in games and contests. ❧ Parents

ainst the other by a child. "Father told me to jump down the well!" "Then you must do it, dear,"

is more valuable in life than a ready wit; the latter may sometimes bring enemies, but the former

hat did you say?" ❧ To be bored is a bad habit. ❧ Don't pretend to know more than you do. ❧

ry foundation upon which social life is built. ❧ Never do anything that is unpleasant to others. ❧

ble if left to their own devices. Even though they may commit no serious offenses, such as making

op this way and that in their chairs, knock spoons and forks together, dawdle over their food, feed

long and rapidly, all in one breath, until they are pink around the eyes, and are literally gasping.

eat without spilling anything or smearing its lips, and drink without making grease "moons" on its

ining-room as a treat, for Sunday lunch or breakfast. . . . But a child that is noisy, that reaches out

ave the nursery before it has been properly graduated. ❧ Snobbish as it sounds and is, a brilliant

lly assorted frumps on the outskirts of society cannot expect to achieve a very distinguished result.

A NOTE ABOUT THE TEXT

Emily Post made up humorous stories to illustrate good (and bad) manners, inventing characters like old Mrs. Toplofty, Mr. Kindhart, Mrs. Wellborn, and Mrs. Worldly. These characters appeared in her 1922 book *Etiquette in society, in business, in politics and at home,* and you'll also meet them in the book you have in your hands.

Certainly not!
Simply figments
of Emily Post's
imagination.

We're not actually
real people, you know . . .

Too true!
Emily invented us
to show examples
of good and bad
behavior in her
etiquette book.

Clever lass!

Thanks a LOT, Emily Post!

WRITTEN BY

Jennifer LaRue Huget

ILLUSTRATED BY

Alexandra Boiger

schwartz & wade books • new york

Everything was just dandy...

till that Emily Post book showed up.

Suddenly it was Emily Post this,
Emily Post that.

We weren't allowed to slump in our chairs.

We had to keep our hands to ourselves.

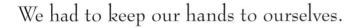

We couldn't shout at the top of our
lungs. In fact, we were allowed to speak
only when spoken to.

Emily Post said we were like little monkeys.
But little monkeys get to have lots more fun.

To make matters worse, Emily Post brought her friends along. Mrs. Worldly. Mrs. Toplofty. Mrs. Wellborn. The Kindharts. They were always hovering around the house, commenting on everything we did.

If we said a cross word, Mother would put her hands on her hips and ask, "Now, do you think Mr. Kindhart would ever say a thing like that?"

"Not if that ol' Emily Post was within earshot," I'd mumble.

We were miserable.

But Mother was not. "One day you'll be glad I introduced you to Emily Post," she said. "We may not be as rich as Mrs. Worldly, and we may not have servants like the Wellborns, but that doesn't mean you children shouldn't have manners fine enough for those Best Society folks."

Best Society? Sounded more like the *worst* society.

Mealtime was unbearable.

No more leaning on our elbows at the table.

We couldn't save time by chewing while chatting.

We couldn't butter our bread the
sensible way.

We couldn't even feed the poor starving dog.

Couldn't,

couldn't,

couldn't!

One afternoon, Mother made me come inside the house, just because I wasn't playing fair with the others. "I bet Emily Post wasn't so perfect when she was a kid," I muttered.

Mrs. Worldly took me aside, patting my shoulder. "Oh, dear, no! Certainly not!" she whispered, glancing at Mother to make sure she wasn't listening. "I heard that when Emily turned three she was given a tin windup toy. She couldn't wait to get her hands on that toy. But her grandfather said, 'No, you might break it! You might hurt your hands!' Emily threw a bit of a tantrum, I'm afraid, and the toy was put up on a shelf. Emily was sent outside to play with another gift, a little china tea set.

"Well, Emily went outside, all right. She smashed that toy china to smithereens. Then she fed the pieces to the goldfish swimming in the fountain! No, dear, Emily certainly wasn't perfect."

"Aha!" I said to myself.
"I knew it!"
But I still didn't like
that Emily Post.

At dinner one evening, I *really* got fed up. Mother had insisted that we speak with one another during the meal. "Emily Post says that at dinner parties, it is absolutely essential that you talk with the person next to you," Mother explained. "Might as well start practicing now."

"But what if we don't feel like talking?" I asked Mrs. Toplofty after I'd helped clear the table.

"Oh, dear, I know what that's like," the old lady said. "Why, at dinner once, I was seated next to a man I detested. So I said to him, 'I shall not talk to you—because I don't care to. But for the sake of my hostess I shall say my multiplication tables. Twice one are two, twice two are four . . .' And I continued on through the tables, making him alternate them with me. As soon as I politely could, I turned again to my other companion."

Gee, I thought. Why can't I come up with a clever plan like that?

Then, one day,
I did.

In the morning, we kids sat quietly at the breakfast table eating our eggs. (Very neatly, holding our forks as if they were pencils.)

"Mother," Big Brother said. "I do believe you should replace those wilting flowers. Emily Post said so."

Mother looked up from her plate, surprised. Then she smiled and said, "Why, of course, dear. I'll attend to it immediately."

Big Brother grinned a tiny grin.

That afternoon, Mother said, "Hush, children. I need to make a phone call!"

"*Telephone,*" Sister corrected. "Emily Post prefers that we say 'telephone.'"

Mother swallowed. "You're absolutely right, darling. Thank you for reminding me."

If we kept this up, Mother'd be as tired of that old Emily Post as we were!

At dinner that evening, I piped up. "Why, Mother, I believe Emily Post would have something to say about this smudgy silverware. You really should polish it, shouldn't you?"

Mother put down her fork with a clink. She frowned. Her cheeks turned red. She narrowed her eyes and glared at each of us, one at a time. We sat up straight, not knowing what would come next.

Finally, Mother cleared her throat. She folded her napkin and laid it on the table. She smiled a big cheery smile. "Yes, my sweet, you are perfectly correct. The silver *is* a terrible mess." We beamed.

Mother cleared her throat again. "In fact," she said, "it's such an embarrassment, I'm sure you won't mind spending tomorrow polishing it till it gleams."

Drat.

But I wasn't giving up.

The next morning, we all got busy. But not with the silver.
When Mother came downstairs, she found Sister strolling around the parlor with a bag of sand on her head, improving her posture. Big Brother was making a long list of things we'd need—a cook, a housemaid, a butler, finger bowls, engraved stationery, turtle soup—if we were going to be like Best Society. I was teaching Baby how a gentleman smokes a pipe.

Mother gasped. "What on earth are you children up to now?"

"Good morning, Mother," Sister said. "Why, we're just trying to please Emily Post. Oh, dear," she added. "You're not wearing that old gray dress *again* today, are you? Emily Post wouldn't approve, you know."

Sand dribbled out of the bag on Sister's head.
Big Brother's hands were all blotchy with ink.
Baby burped.
Mother grimaced.
"That does it." Mother stamped her foot.
Then she stormed out of the room.

We heard her bedroom door slam.
She was gone a long time.
We started to wonder whether she'd *ever* come back.

When she did, she wasn't alone. Mrs. Worldly and the others trailed behind her.

"Thank you so much for all your help," Mother said as she threw open the front door. "We do hope you've enjoyed your stay. And here—don't forget this!" she added, tucking the big blue book under Mrs. Worldly's arm as she guided her out the door.

"Ta-ta!" we all cried, waving our hankies.

And everything was just dandy again, once that Emily Post book went away.

Meet Emily Post

RULES OF ETIQUETTE ARE NOTHING MORE THAN SIGN-POSTS BY WHICH WE ARE GUIDED TO THE GOAL OF GOOD TASTE. Emily Price was born in Baltimore in 1873. Her rich family belonged to what was known in the late 1800s as America's Best Society. In Best Society, there were strict rules about how to behave in every social situation.

Emily dreamed of becoming an architect, like her father. But women in Best Society didn't usually have careers. They spent their days socializing, doing charity work, and managing their households. Emily didn't really need a job, anyway, especially after she married Edwin Post, a promising young businessman. Emily ended up becoming a writer, a creative job she could do at home.

In the early 1920s, an editor asked Emily to write a book about etiquette. People across America were eager to learn how to act like members of Best Society—and to teach their children to behave that way, too.

But Emily Post didn't *want* to write about etiquette. Etiquette books were prim and picky. Worse yet, they usually were written by people who'd never been part of Best Society, and they got everything all wrong!

Emily decided to write a different kind of etiquette book. She taught her readers that etiquette wasn't just about following specific rules, like which fork to use, but about treating other people with respect, kindness, consideration, and honesty.

Unlike other etiquette experts, Emily Post didn't preach. She made up humorous stories to illustrate good (and bad) behavior, inventing characters with names like Old Mrs. Toplofty, Mr. Kindhart, Mrs. Wellborn, and Mrs. Worldly.

Etiquette in society, in business, in politics and at home was an instant bestseller when it was published in 1922. The blue, 627-page, four-dollar book quickly became known not by its full title but simply by its author's name.

But even Emily needed etiquette advice sometimes. One day she asked a clerk at Tiffany's (a fancy store in New York City) for help in choosing the right words for an invitation. Not recognizing his customer, the gentleman agreed to help. He reached under the counter—and pulled out a copy of "Emily Post"!

Emily Post died in 1960. While she wasn't the first—or the last—person to write about etiquette, she did more to spread good manners across America than anyone before or since. Today the Emily Post Institute, which she started in 1946, continues her work by answering people's etiquette questions and publishing updated etiquette books.

So if your folks are always after you to mind your manners, you probably have Emily Post to thank.

Thanks a lot! to the beloved characters in my life:
my kids, Sophie and Charlie; my husband, Kirby;
and my parents, Thelma and Charles

—*J.L.H.*

To Vanessa, mein Augenstern

—*A.B.*

Text copyright © 2009 by Jennifer LaRue Huget
Illustrations copyright © 2009 by Alexandra Boiger
All rights reserved.
Published in the United States by Schwartz & Wade Books, an imprint of Random House Children's Books,
a division of Random House, Inc., New York.
Schwartz & Wade Books and the colophon are trademarks of Random House, Inc.
Visit us on the Web! www.randomhouse.com/kids
Educators and librarians, for a variety of teaching tools, visit us at www.randomhouse.com/teachers

Library of Congress Cataloging-in-Publication Data
Huget, Jennifer LaRue.
Thanks a lot, Emily Post! / Jennifer LaRue Huget ; illustrated by Alexandra Boiger. — 1st ed.
p. cm.
Summary: When a mother instructs her children to behave according to Emily Post's rules of etiquette, they respond by insisting that Mother follow
the rules, as well. Includes information about Post and selected items from her 1922 book.
ISBN 978-0-375-83853-8 (trade) — ISBN 978-0-375-93853-5 (Gibraltar lib. bdg.)
[1. Etiquette—Fiction. 2. Conduct of life—Fiction. 3. Mothers—Fiction. 4. Post, Emily, 1873–1960. Etiquette.]
I. Boiger, Alexandra, ill. II. Title.

PZ7.H872958Thc 2009
[E]—dc22
2008004994

PRINTED IN CHINA
10 9 8 7 6 5 4 3 2 1
First Edition

EMILY POST'S GUIDE TO GOOD (AND BAD) BEHAVIOR: *To sit gracefully one should not per*
yourself!" might almost be put at the head of the first chapter of every book on etiquette. *Do n*
but there should be a feeling of strength and warmth in the clasp, and, as in bowing, one should a
creates a feeling of liking or of irritation between two strangers. Who does not dislike a "boneless" l
is not at all like a court with an especial queen or king, nor is it confined to any one place or group,
globe, the members of which are invariably people of cultivation and worldly knowledge, who have n
Bread should always be broken into small pieces with the fingers before being eaten. . . . . Bread
are made to avoid ugliness; to let any one see what you have in your mouth is repulsive; to mak
manners always keep their places at table neat. People with disgusting manners get everything in d
as you can, and leave the rest on your plate. *One inexorable rule of etiquette is that you must*
girl (or boy) giving a party should receive with her mother at the door and greet all her friends as th
On no account must she be allowed to tell a child "I hate dolls," if a friend has brought her one. S
want the best toys in the grab-bag or scream because another child gets the prize that is offered in
appearance, taste and character. *One who can not help sulking, or explaining, or protesting wh*
must never disagree before the children. It simply can't be! Nor can there be an appeal to one paren
is the mother's only possible comment. *As a possession for either woman or man, a ready sm*
always brings friends. *When some one is talking to you, it is inconsiderate to keep repeating*
Consideration for the rights and feelings of others is not merely a rule for behavior in public but th
Girls are usually daintier and more easily taught than boys, but most children will behave badly d
a mess of their food or themselves, or talking with their mouths full, all children love to crumb brea
animals—if any are allowed in the room—or become restless and noisy. *Children like to drink*
They also love to put their whole hands in their finger-bowls and wiggle their fingers. *When it*
mug or tumbler (by always wiping its mouth before drinking), it may be allowed to come to table in t
to help itself to candy or cake, that interrupts the conversation, that eats untidily has been allowed
ball is necessarily a collection of brilliantly fashionable people, and the hostess who gathers in all th